1

First published: January 2019

ISBN (Hard Cover): 978-1-943413-10-2
ISBN (Soft Cover): 978-1-943413-11-9

Visit us on the web!
www.tozknows.com

In addition to promoting literacy and biblical education to children, Toz Knows partners with non-profit and other charity organizations to give back to the community. For every TWO Toz Knows books purchased, ONE is donated to a child in need.

For more information regarding a partnership with Toz Knows, visit
www.tozknows.com/partners

Printed in the United States of America

Illustrator: Tina Modugno
www.tinamodugno.com

Toz Knows Elijah

Mindi Jo Furby & Kaci Hollingsworth

Illustrated by Tina Modugno

3

The sirens were blaring
A tornado was tearing
Its way through the town
Spreading panic around.

When Toz and Miley heard the sound,
They rushed home from the playground.
Daddy Blue shut the door
And they crouched together on the floor.

Wind was making the house creak
So Toz decided to take a peek
Under the crack of the door—
The house was shaking to its core.

As the sirens continued to blare
They started getting really scared.
Not knowing what was ahead
Filled their hearts with lots of dread.

Then Daddy Blue began to pray
For God to have His sovereign way.
God was more powerful than a storm—
He could keep them all from harm.

But if He didn't, that'd be ok
His love for them would never change.
They'd soon know what God would do,
And would trust Him through and through.

Just then the White Bird flew down
Taking Tozer to another town.
They headed quickly back in time
To see God's power fill the sky.

Long ago few believed
Because of Ahab, a corrupt king.
He worshipped idols instead of God
And proved to be a total fraud.

12

But not all followed his wicked ways
Some remained faithful all of their days.
Elijah was one who stood his ground
And hoped to bring others around.

Because of wickedness in the land
God took action; He made a stand.
He caused a drought; the land was dry
For years no rain fell from the sky.
But God would reverse this stance of power,
After a showdown, He'd send a rain shower.

Elijah told Ahab to gather the people
To come and see God had no equal.
To Mount Carmel they would head
And see how far they'd been misled.

They'd each prepare an ox and build an altar
The true God would stand, the other would falter.
Whichever God called fire down
Would show the truth to the town.

The false prophets were first to go,
And oh, did they put on a show.
They hurt themselves and danced and prayed
But their god was silent because he was fake.

18

Around noon Elijah began to tease
"Maybe your god is just asleep!
Or perhaps he's gone on a little quest
Be louder so he can hear your request!"

The prophets continued but the silence remained;
Elijah told them to quit when evening came.
He then told the people to come near
For the true God would soon become clear.

Twelve stones formed his altar to the Lord
His faith would soon see a reward.
Around the altar he dug a trench
And ordered that it all be drenched.

Four pitchers of water were poured on top
Not once or twice, but three times sopped.
Some people were probably most confused,
While others must've stood amused.
The point was to burn the ox offering,
But water would make that a difficult thing!

Elijah wasn't the least concerned
To God his attention was fully turned.
He then prayed to God most high
To send down fire from the sky
To prove that He was real and strong
And He had been there all along.

When the people saw that display of power,
They worshipped God in a humbled cower.
All the false prophets went away that day
They'd no longer lead God's people astray.

Elijah then said it would rain
And had his servant look away.
He looked to the sea to watch for a sign
But kept seeing nothing but blue in the sky.

The seventh time the servant glanced
He saw a cloud no bigger than a hand.
Soon the rain came hurling down
The drought was over, a storm came loud.

Suddenly the White Bird took Tozer back
To his family, all tightly packed.
The tornado passed and did a lot of damage
But they were safe, which was all that mattered.

Toz learned a big lesson that day:
God's power is endless and often on display.
He controls weather and all other things,
And listens to prayers of those who believe.

MEET THE TEAM!

Mindi Jo Furby
Author / Publicist

Mindi Jo Furby is an author and speaker who decicates her life to fighting biblical illiteracy one publication at a time. Equipped with a degree in Biblical Studies and a Masters in Religion, she loves helping others fall in love with God through the pages of His Word. She, her husband, and daughters make their home near Hilton Head, SC.

www.mindijofurby.com

Kaci Ann Hollingsworth
Non-Profit Coordinator

Kaci Ann Hollingsworth is also a UNC Chapel Hill grad who loves non-profit organizations and initiatives. She currently works for a non-profit and volunteers with many others. She makes her home with her pup, Mackey, in Hilton Head Island, SC.

Tina Modugno
Children's Illustrator

Tina Modugno is an illustrator, author and publicist from Quebec, Canada. She has illustrated and published many titles including some of her own children's books. Tina is a huge animal advocate and lives with five feline family members. She is the creator of *"The Oreo Cat"* and through her work, she is dedicated to helping educate the public about the crippling side effects of feline declawing.

www.tinamodugno.com
www.theoreocat.com